Most nights this book can be found on

my_____

bookshelf....

unless some thing decided to hide it in
my closet, or perhaps just under my bed?

Flyin Lion and Friends

Monsters Don't Scare Me, Very Much

 By: David Arnold

CITATION MEDIA

Monsters don't scare me during the day but some nights I have to say when I'm alone and in the dark, I sometimes find that I'm afraid.

Just yesterday
as darkness fell,
and I was snuggled in my bed, I'm sure
I saw a shadow over there where some
thing lurked behind my chair.

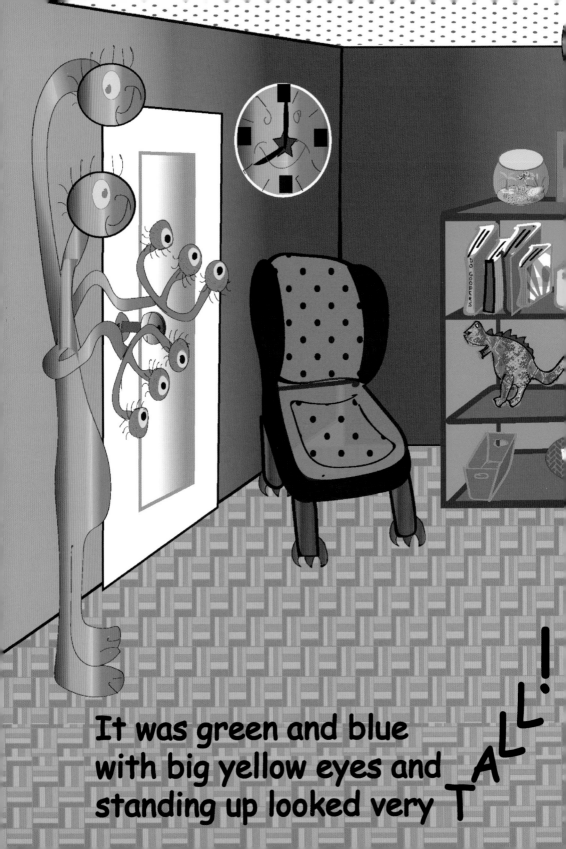

It was green and blue
with big yellow eyes and
standing up looked very T_A^LL!

When suddenly to my surprise it grinned at me just like the clock up on my wall.

I am sure that it was not alone
as moments later I heard a groan
beneath my bed and so I said out
loud and as bravely as I dared:

'Whatever you
   are, please just stay down there,
   so I won't have to be so scared'

Moaning and thumping
eerily and frightening
me all too easily.

I'm sure its trying to climb up and join me in a pillow fight before I can fall asleep tonight.

So like I said 'Monsters',
they don't scare me very much

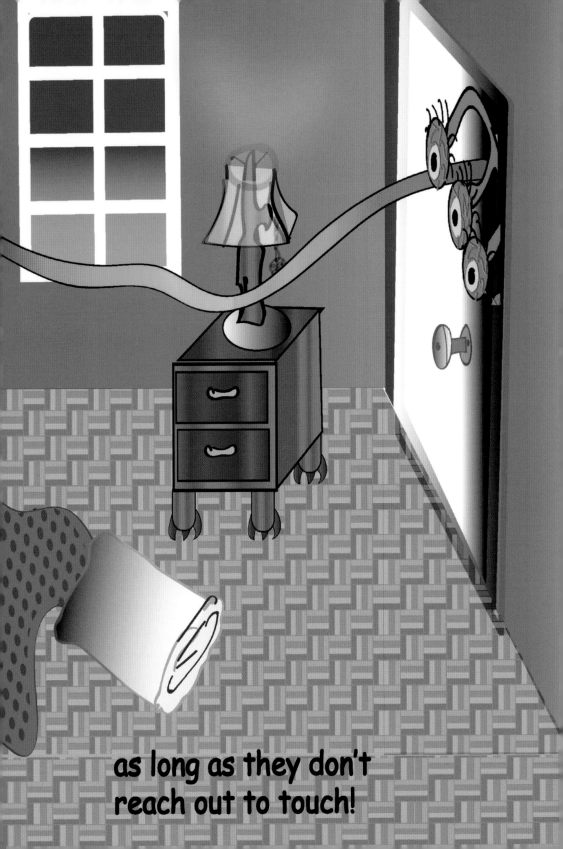

as long as they don't
reach out to touch!

Their touch would scare me wide awake
and under the covers I would shake....

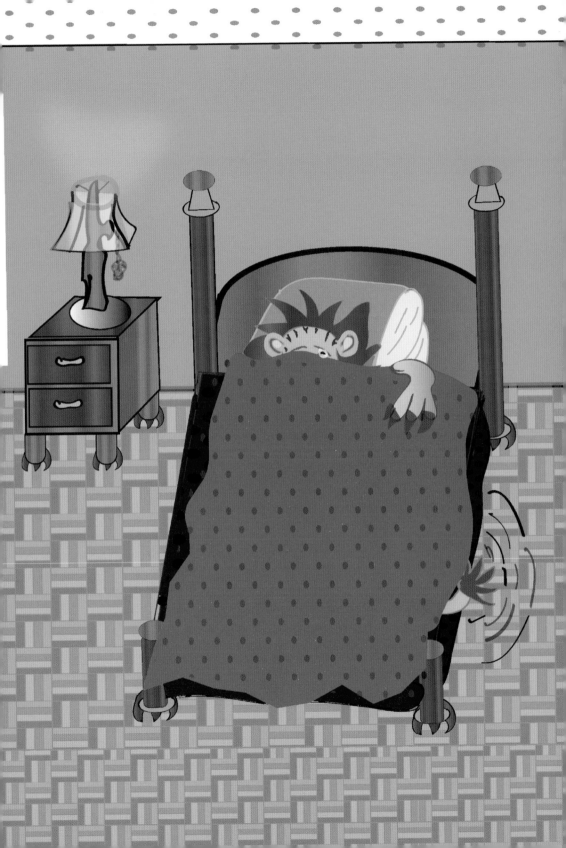

Hiding from all their fright and scary especially the ones that are really hairy.

Or if they have three extra feet
oh my how they give me the creeps.

All alone here in my bed with my
covers pulled from my toes to head.

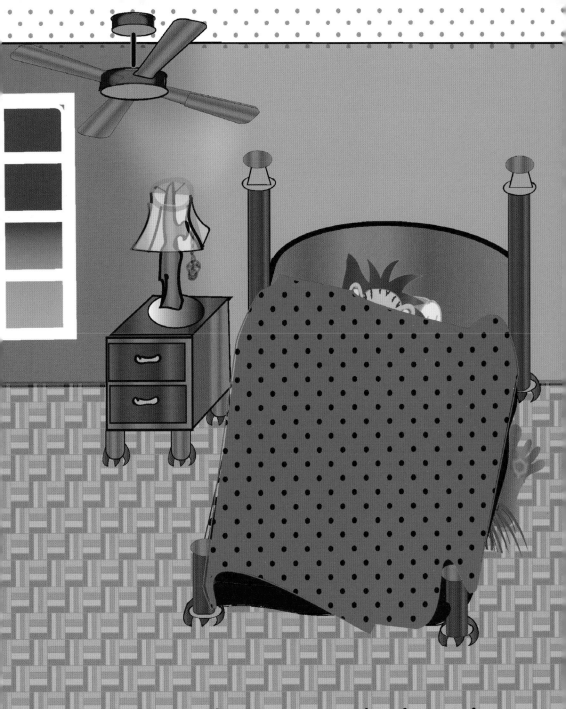

Trying not to make a peep which might disturb what's underneath and keeping e from my sleep.

My parents say don't
be afraid of a shadow
on the wall or a squeak
made by my bed.

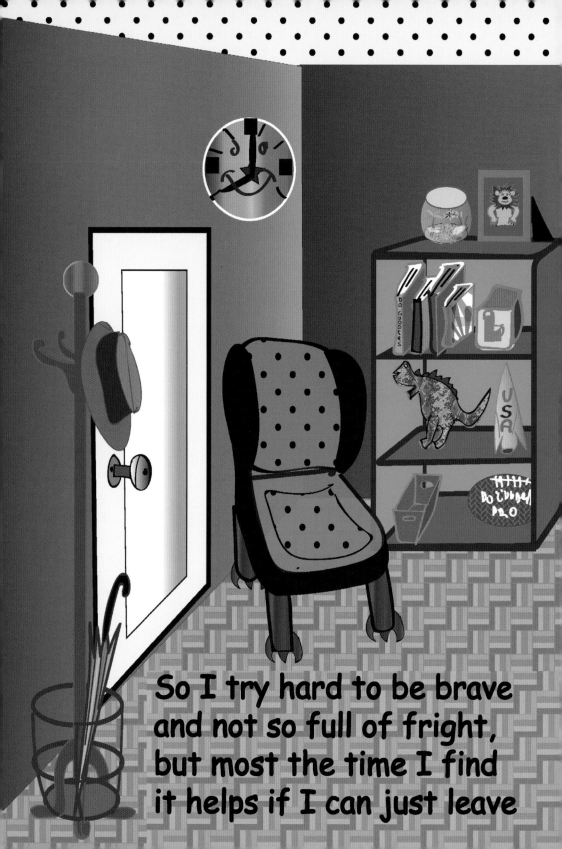

So I try hard to be brave
and not so full of fright,
but most the time I find
it helps if I can just leave

ON a LIGHT!

Just then my mom comes
in to say 'good night' so I ask
her if she might read a story

That I like about
all the monsters
I'm imagining
TONIGHT!

Moments later I'm tucked into bed and mom kisses my cheek as now it seems I'm fast asleep.

There will be no monsters in my dreams tonight, but if I should wake before daylight

know that I will be all right as soon
as I can make it down the hall and
into my parent's bed I crawl.

Citation Media
For Inquiries, call 845-469-8605

Copyright 2018 Citation Media
Published by Citation Media LLC
91 Odyssey Drive
Chester, NY 10918

Printed in China

ISBN-10: 0-9992986-1-5

ISBN-13: 978-0-9992986-1-9

1C M18 1

CEO Charlotte Bonhard

Written & Illustrated by: David Arnold

CITATION MEDIA

Flyin Lion and Friends

I'm a Flyin' Lion,
You'll never catch me cryin...;
When things go wrong,
I just sing my song and
It makes me strong,
Cause I'm a Flyin' Lion,
I'll always keep on smilin'
Cause I'm a Flyin' Lion,
I'll always keep on tryin'
You'll NEVER catch me cryin!

'Animal ABCs'

Ultimate Unicorns drink rainbow water
From pure mountain streams & they
Usually can only be seen in your dreams.

'Lottamus Hippopotamus'

2 Hippopotamus if we add another,
perhaps he might be number one's little brother?

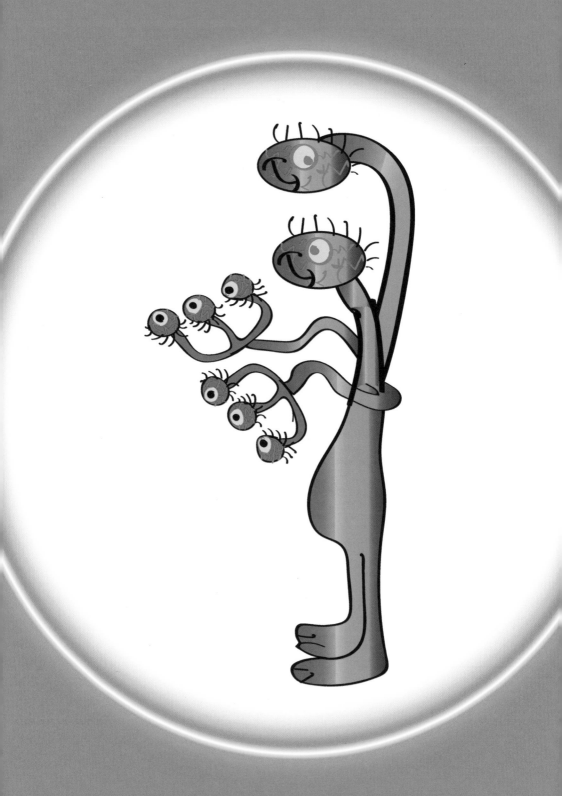